The Gift of the Crocodile

A Cinderella Story

By Judy Sierra

Illustrated by Reynold Ruffins

SIMON & SCHUSTER BOOKS FOR YOUNG READERS

NEW YORK LONDON TORONTO SYDNEY SINGAPORE

SIMON & SCHUSTER BOOKS FOR YOUNG READERS
An imprint of Simon & Schuster Children's Publishing Division
1230 Avenue of the Americas, New York, New York 10020

The text of this book is set in Elysium Book.
The illustrations are rendered in acrylic on watercolor paper.
Printed in Hong Kong
10 9 8 7 6 5 4 3 2 1

Library of Congress Cataloging-in-Publication Data

Sierra, Judy.
The gift of the crocodile : a Cinderella story / by Judy Sierra; illustrated by
Reynold Ruffins. — 1st ed.
p. cm.
Summary: In this Indonesian version of the Cinderella story, a girl named
Damura escapes her cruel stepmother and stepsister and marries a handsome
prince with the help of Grandmother Crocodile.
ISBN 0-689-82188-3
[1. Fairy tales. 2. Folklore—Indonesia.] I. Ruffins, Reynold, ill. II. Title.
PZ8.S34558Gr 2000
398.2'09598'02—dc21
98-40592
CIP

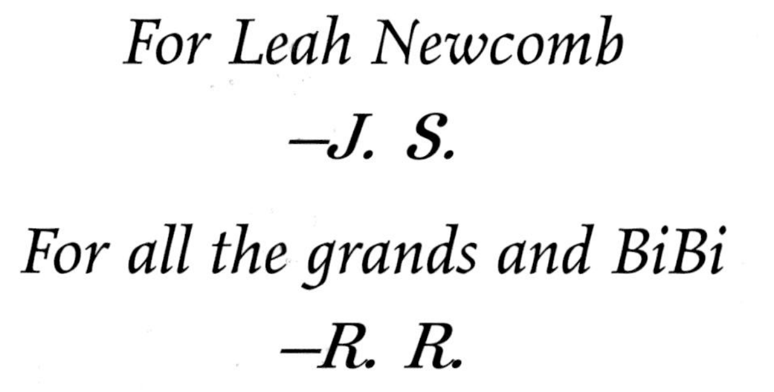

For Leah Newcomb

–J. S.

For all the grands and BiBi

–R. R.

In the Spice Islands, where clove and nutmeg trees grow, a girl named Damura lived long ago. Damura's mother taught her to kindle a fire and cook, to tend and harvest rice plants, and to dance the graceful dances of their ancestors.

There came a time when Damura's mother grew weak and she knew she would not live much longer. So she called the girl to her bedside and reminded her to respect all wild creatures, for they would help and comfort her. Later, when Damura missed her mother, she would talk to the lorikeet and the little green parrot who came to perch on the nutmeg trees.

A widow who lived in their village took a liking to Damura's father. She made a pretty doll for the girl. "Would you like this?" she asked. Yes, Damura wanted the doll more than anything she had ever seen. "You may have it," the woman said, "if you tell your father that he should marry me."

Damura hugged the doll and hurried home. "Please," she begged, "will you marry the neighbor woman? She is so nice."

"We have a good enough life," her father said. But Damura insisted, and finally he agreed to marry.

The stepmother came to their home with a daughter of her own. At first the two of them were kind to Damura, but soon enough, they made her their servant. Every morning Damura arose before dawn, kindled the fire, and cooked. Then she tidied the house and pulled weeds from the rice fields. When the lorikeet and the little green parrot came to talk to Damura, the stepmother shooed them away. At night, Damura slept on the floor amid the cold ashes of the hearth and cried because she had traded her happiness for a doll.

One day, as Damura knelt by the river washing the family's clothes, the current swept away her old ragged sarong. Damura was afraid to return home without it, and she began to cry. Then she remembered her mother's advice. "Creatures of the wild, help me," she called out. Slowly, an ancient crocodile arose from the river and stepped onto the rocks. Damura showed no fear. "Good morning, Grandmother," she said.

"It was wise of you to call me 'Grandmother,' " the crocodile replied, "for if you had not, I might have eaten you. Why are you crying?"

"My sarong has disappeared into the river," Damura told her.

"I will get it for you if you will watch my little one," the crocodile said. Damura saw a tiny crocodile in the water. She lifted it up, but it began to bite her with its sharp teeth. She found a soft twig for it to chew, then she rocked it gently and sang,

"Rockabye, little baby crocodile,
You smell like . . ."

Damura almost said what the baby *really* smelled like, but she remembered her mother's words and sang,

"Rockabye, little baby crocodile,
You smell sweet like the nutmeg tree."

Grandmother Crocodile splashed out of the water, holding in her mouth a silver sarong that sparkled like the night sky.

"That is not my sarong." Damura sighed. "Mine is old and torn."

"This is the one you deserve," the crocodile told her. "Take it, and come see me again if you ever need anything."

When the stepmother saw Damura's beautiful sarong, she took it away and forced the girl to tell how she got it. Next morning, her own daughter went to the river, tossed an old rag into the swift current, and pretended to cry.

Up rose the ancient crocodile. "Good morning, Grandmother," said the stepsister, for Damura had warned her to be polite.

"It is a good thing, child, that you called me 'Grandmother.' Otherwise, I might have eaten you. Why are you crying?"

"I was washing clothes," the stepsister lied. "My sarong floated away, and I can't seem to find it anywhere."

"I will get it for you," said the crocodile. "Just watch my little one while I am gone."

The stepsister picked up the baby crocodile. When it bit her with its sharp teeth, she spanked it and sang,

"Shut your mouth, stinky crocodile,
You smell just like a garbage pile."

Grandmother Crocodile appeared, carrying a sparkling silver cloth. "Is this your sarong?" she asked.

"Give it to me!" the girl shouted. She grabbed it and wrapped it around her waist. Instantly it became a filthy rag swarming with leeches. The girl tried to pull it off, but it stuck to her like glue. Home she ran, howling and weeping.

A year passed, several years passed. One day the houses in the village buzzed with excitement, for the prince had invited all the young women to dance at the palace. He would choose the loveliest as his bride.

"Stepmother, may I wear my silver sarong?" Damura asked.

"Ha! As if a prince would ever look at a dirty thing like you! Your sister shall wear the silver dress. You stay here and tidy up the house."

When the two of them had gone, Damura hurried to the river. "Grandmother! Grandmother!" she called.

"What is it, child?"

"I want so much to go to the palace and dance for the prince," Damura sobbed, "but my stepmother made me stay home. Even if I could go, I have nothing to wear."

The crocodile sank into the water and soon reappeared with a sarong and blouse of pure gold, and slippers to match. "Leave the palace as soon as the first rooster crows," the crocodile warned her, "and remember to return everything to me before you go home."

Then a shining carriage appeared, pulled by a white horse. Damura climbed up and took the reins, and before she could draw a breath, she found herself at the palace gates. Everyone turned and stared at her. They whispered that she surely must be a princess from across the sea. And when the prince saw her dance, using the steps her mother had taught her, he knew that she would be his bride.

Damura wished the night would never end, but as soon as she heard a rooster crow, she ran to her carriage, with the prince at her heels. He tried to climb up after her, but she pushed him away. As he fell back, he caught hold of one of her golden slippers.

"I am sorry," Damura told Grandmother Crocodile when she reached the river. "I have lost a slipper."

"You needn't be sorry. That one slipper will make you a princess."

The next morning a messenger arrived at Damura's village asking that all the young women come at once, for the prince had vowed to find and marry the young woman whom the slipper fit. Damura, dressed in rags, went to the palace with the others.

The prince tried the slipper on each one, but always it was too small. At last he came to Damura. "You needn't try it on *her*," said the stepsister. "She is only my servant." But the slipper fairly flew onto Damura's foot, and it fit perfectly.

"This girl is so shabby," said the prince's counselor. "Even though the slipper fits, you don't have to marry her."

"Rich or poor," the prince declared, "she is my choice."

Damura ran to the river to ask Grandmother Crocodile for her golden clothes and carriage, and when she reappeared she was as beautiful as she had been the evening before. The wedding celebration was the most splendid ever seen, and afterward Damura lived in the palace as a princess should.

Damura's stepmother and stepsister were eaten up with jealousy. A few days after the wedding they arrived, saying sweetly, "We are *so* sorry for the way we treated you, Damura. Let's take a boat ride on the river and become friends again."

Damura agreed, for she thought they had changed their ways, but when the boat reached the middle of the river, they pushed her overboard. Before she could draw a breath, she was swallowed by a crocodile. The two women paddled back to shore and ran to the palace shouting, "Damura has fallen into the river. A crocodile has swallowed her!" They hoped that the prince would soon forget her and marry the stepsister.

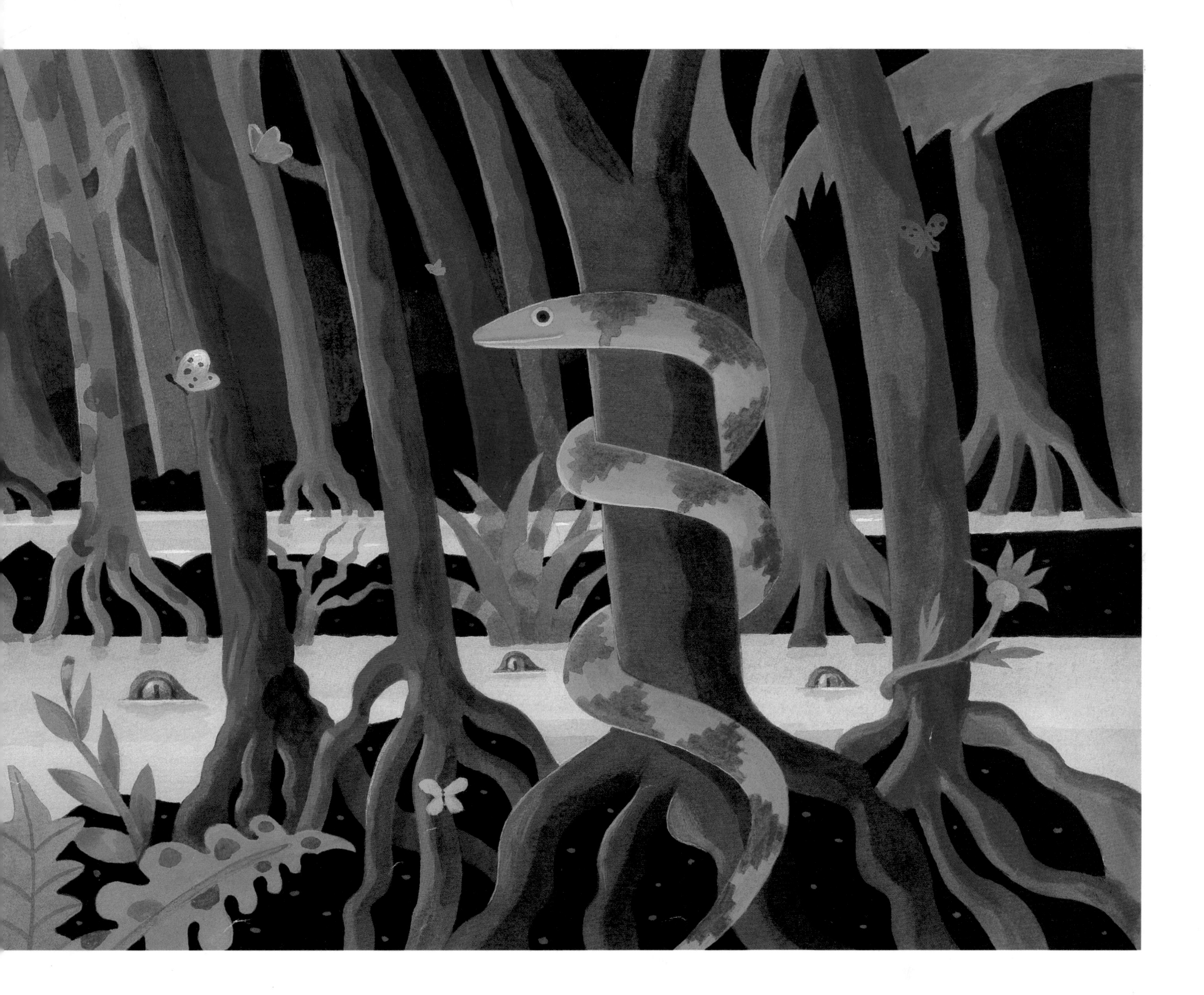

The prince went at once to the riverbank and shouted, "Grandmother! Grandmother!"

The great creature appeared and swam toward him. "Why have you come here?" she asked.

"Princess Damura has been eaten by a crocodile," he cried.

Grandmother Crocodile thrashed her tail in anger. She called together all her river-children and asked, "Which one of you dared eat my precious grandchild?"

There was a long silence, then a fat young crocodile confessed, "It was me. I did it."

"Spit her out right now!" commanded Grandmother Crocodile. She licked Damura's face and brought her back to life. "None of you shall ever touch Damura again, or her husband, or their children," she commanded. "But if you see her stepmother or stepsister, you must eat them at once!"

The stepmother and stepsister were hiding nearby, and when they heard Grandmother Crocodile's words, they fled into the darkest part of the forest never to be seen again.

Damura and her prince returned to the palace, where they lived for many years in great splendor and happiness. Their children splashed in the river, and talked to the lorikeet and the little green parrot, and played in the shade of the clove and nutmeg trees.

Folklore Note

This tale is from the island of Halmahera in the Moluccas, or Spice Islands, in Indonesia. The Spice Islands was the destination of Christopher Columbus when he began his historic voyage in 1492. Until that time, clove trees grew nowhere else in the world. Yet because cloves have been found in the ruins of Mesopotamia and ancient Rome, we know that trade between the Moluccas and the Mediterranean began at least three thousand years ago. Spice traders no doubt carried stories as well as spices; perhaps they helped spread Cinderella tales, too. No one knows, though, exactly where these tales originated. The earliest written version of a Cinderella tale is from China.

The Gift of the Crocodile contains folktale motifs found in Cinderella tales from other parts of the world. In many versions, the heroine loses something at a river and finds a magical helper there. The helper might be a fairy, a bird, a crab, or a crocodile (a crocodile also plays the role of fairy godmother in tales from the Philippines). In versions like the Appalachian Cinderella story, *Ashpet,* as in *The Gift of the Crocodile,* the stepmother and stepsister torment the heroine even more cruelly after she has married the prince. The motif of the lost slipper is, of course, very widespread. Folktale detectives should be able to find other familiar Cinderella motifs in *The Gift of the Crocodile.*

The Gift of the Crocodile was collected and retold around 1900 by G. J. Ellen, a missionary, and was published in 1916 in *Woordenlijst van het Pagoe op Noord-Halmahera.*